The Tale of the Tooth Fairy

igloobooks

Daisy and Elliot had both lost their very first teeth. "Do you think the tooth fairy will visit?" asked Daisy excitedly, looking out of the window at the glistening, silver moon.

"Fairies aren't real," said Elliot, giggling. Just then,
a shooting star whooshed across the sky, leaving a glittering
trail behind. Magic bursts of stardust shimmered all around.

All along the chimney pots, over the pale,
moonlit rooftops, came the tinkle of tiny bells.
In a sparkling swirl a fairy flew, fluttering
this way and that.

Her glittering wand waved a magical trail.
The tooth fairy had come to call.

"I've come to take you on a magical adventure," said the
tooth fairy, as she swished her sparkling wand.

A puff of magical fairy dust circled Daisy and Elliot.
Daisy looked behind her. "We've got fairy wings!" she cried.

With a whoosh, the children fluttered up,
up and into the twinkling sky. They swooped
among moonbeams and soared past stars
that glinted like jewels.

Then, with a soft swoosh, Daisy, Elliot and the tooth fairy landed in a meadow. Little fairies fluttered and cheered as bells tinkled everywhere. "Welcome to Fairyland!" they sang.

"When a tooth falls out, we do something amazingly magical with it," explained the tooth fairy. "Follow me and I will show you," she said, fluttering into the forest.

In a clearing, a beautiful tower shimmered in the sunlight.
"This is where teeth turn into magic fairy dust," said the
tooth fairy. "It makes wishes come true."

Sparklewing, the fairy-dust fairy, swished her wand
and golden sparkles flew through the air. POOF!

Pearly teeth turned into fairy dust. "Ta-dah!" cried Sparklewing
proudly, as she collected the precious dust in little bottles.

Next, the tooth fairy took Daisy and Elliot to a magical meadow filled with sweet-smelling flowers. "This is our enchanted flower garden," the tooth fairy explained. "The teeth have a special job here, too."

Petal, the flower fairy, planted a tooth into the soft
soil and waved her magic wand. Suddenly, a beautiful
flower sprung up and the excited fairies cheered
and danced around in delight.

Daisy, Elliot and the tooth fairy
reached an enchanted spring.
Sparkling water shimmered with
magic, as excited fairies fluttered
around the pool.

Rainsparkle, the rainbow fairy, tossed a tooth into
the spring. With a swish of her wand, an amazing rainbow
burst out from the water and arched across the sky.

Fairy Palace

Soon, the sun had set. "What will our
teeth be used for?" asked Daisy, curiously.
"Follow me," said the tooth fairy, smiling.
"I've saved the best until last."

As they fluttered deep into the
forest, the enchanting fairy palace sparkled
brightly in the distance for all to see.

"I've been waiting for your visit," said the fairy queen, with a voice as sweet as honey. Then she took the teeth from Daisy and Elliot.

With a swish of her wand, the teeth turned into two sparkling stars. Whoosh! Up they flew, shining brighter than any star they'd ever seen.

"It's time for you to go back now," said the fairy queen. "Here's a special golden coin for you to remember us by." She swished her glistening wand and suddenly, Fairyland began to shimmer.

Before they knew it, Daisy and Elliot were safely back home. "Look!" cried Daisy, as she looked out of the window. "Our stars are shining brightly."